Bippity Bop Barbershop

by **Natasha Anastasia Tarpley**

Illustrated by **E. B. Lewis**

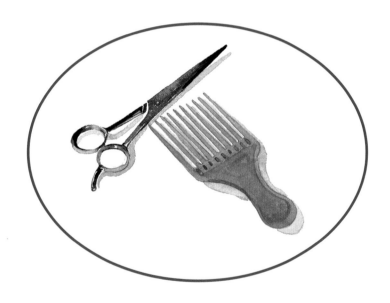

Megan Tingley Books

LITTLE, BROWN AND COMPANY

New York   Boston

For my brother, Omar,
one of the bravest men I know
—N. A. T.

To my friend Wadud Ahmad
—E. B. L.

Little, Brown and Company

Hachette Book Group
1290 Avenue of the Americas, New York, NY 10104
Visit our website at www.lb-kids.com

Little, Brown and Company is a division of the Hachette Book Group, Inc.
The Little, Brown name and logo are trademarks of Hachette Book Group, Inc.

The publisher is not responsible for websites (or their content) that are not owned by the publisher.

First Paperback Edition: January 2009
First published in hardcover in February 2002 by Little, Brown and Company

Library of Congress Cataloging-in-Publication Data

Tarpley, Natasha.
  Bippity bop barbershop/ by Natasha Anastasia Tarpley ; illustrated by E. B. Lewis. —1st ed.
    p. cm.
  "Megan Tingley books."
  Summary: A story celebrating a young African-American boy's first trip to the barbershop.
  ISBN 978-0-316-52284-7 (hc) / ISBN 978-0-316-03382-4 (pb)
  [1. Barbershop—Fiction.   2. Haircutting—Fiction.   3. Fathers and sons—Fiction.   4. Afro-Americans—Fiction.]
1. Lewis, Earl B., ill.   II. Title.

PZ7.T176 Bar 2002
[E]—dc21   00-030188

20 19 18 17 16

APS

Printed in China

The illustrations for this book were done in watercolor on Arches 300 pound paper.
The text was set in Leawood, and the display type is Barmeno.

Author's Note

I wore my hair in a short natural—about an inch long all around—for several years. My brother, Omar, usually cut my hair. When Omar was busy, I went to the barbershop. Most times, I was one of only a couple women there. And while everyone was polite, I stayed on the outskirts of the special space that the men seemed to enter as soon as they walked into the shop. I noticed the way their chests swelled as they boasted of a promotion or a new baby. I noticed the softness in their eyes when they talked about the women in their lives; the way their fingers jabbed the air when they made a point in a heated discussion; the way they folded their hands quietly in their laps as they sat thinking.

Sometimes a little boy would come in to get his hair cut for the first time. The boy's father and the other men would do their best to make him feel comfortable and brave. It was a rite of passage, for once completed, the boy was welcomed into the fold, his spot among the men now secured. I was reminded of the special time my mother and I shared as she combed my hair. I saw the same gentleness, the same comfort, the same easy laughter flowing between them like water.

There is something magical about the rituals surrounding our hair. Just as my first picture book, *I Love My Hair!*, sought to capture this tender bond between mother and daughter, *Bippity Bop Barbershop* celebrates the unique sharing I witnessed between father and son and among the men in the barbershop. These books are dedicated to the sacred spaces we create for one another, where we lay down our guards and defenses and lay our hands on each other's hearts, revealing and reveling in our unique beauty. Let us continue to create more of these spaces in every aspect of our lives.

Peace and blessings.

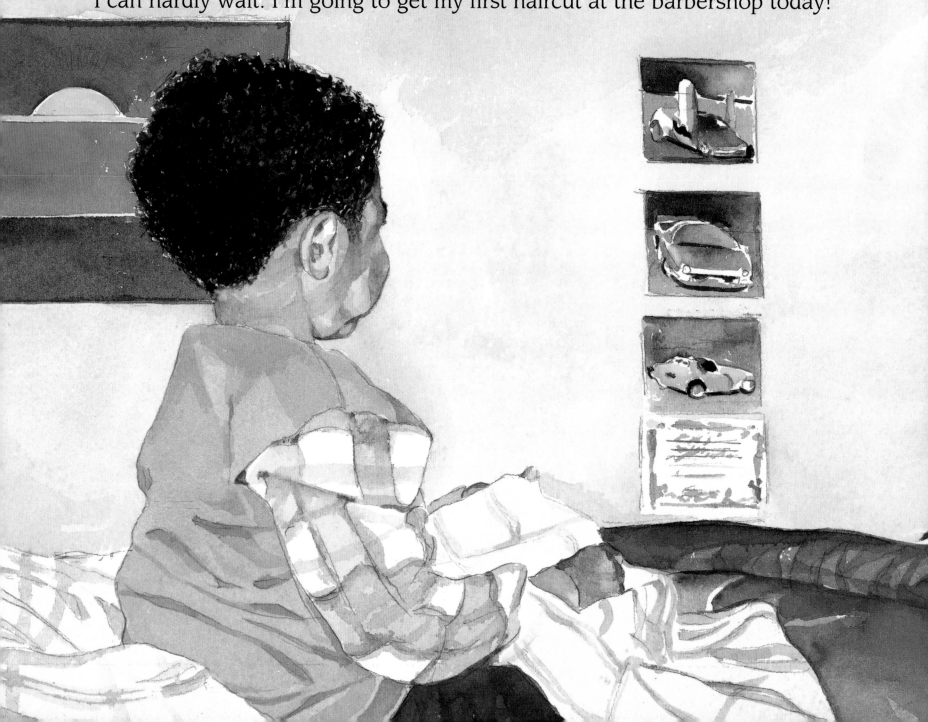

Early Saturday morning, Daddy comes to wake me with our secret knock.
Bippity-be-bop-bop! Bippity-be-bop-bop!
"You up, Little Man?" Daddy pokes his head into my room.
"I'm up!" I say excitedly and jump out of bed.
I can hardly wait. I'm going to get my first haircut at the barbershop today!

Mama and my sister, Keyana, are still asleep.
Daddy and I have the house all to ourselves.

Quietly, Daddy and I dress in matching blue jeans
and gym shoes, then head outside.

We turn onto Main Street and stop at Jack's Sweet Shop. Daddy orders a gooey cinnamon roll and black coffee, and a glazed doughnut and chocolate milk for me. "Miles is getting his first haircut at the barbershop today," Daddy tells Mr. J. "Is that so?" Mr. J asks, leaning over the counter. I nod yes. "This calls for a celebration. I'll make your milk a double." Mr. J pours chocolate milk into a tall cup. "Be brave, Little Man," he says as he hands it to me.

We eat as we walk. Up ahead I see the green and yellow awning and the white letters on the window that say SEYMOUR'S BARBERSHOP. Next to the door is a short, white barber's pole. It has red stripes, which curl and swirl around it like strange fish swimming in a sea of white.

And there's Mr. Seymour in the window, with his wild, gray hair, dusting off his big, shiny chair.

Mr. Seymour has been Daddy's barber since Daddy was a kid like me. Now, he'll be my barber, too.

Inside, the shop is crowded.
Daddy stops to whisper something to Mr. Seymour,
and then we walk to the back of the shop to find a seat.
"Hey there, Charles!" "Hey there, Little Man!" "What's going on?"
people call out as we pass.
"First haircut?" one of the men asks me. I nod yes.
"Nothing to it," he says. "Just gotta be brave."

All these people are telling me to be brave,
but I don't know exactly what they mean.
"What does 'brave' mean, Daddy?" I ask.
"It just means that you're not afraid," Daddy says.
When we sit down, I practice being brave.

As Daddy and I wait our turn, we watch two men playing checkers.
Slap! One of the men slams his checker on the board.
"King me!" he shouts with his arms raised high.

Another group of men is clustered around the television at the back of the shop watching a basketball game. "Come on, man, shoot the ball! What're you waiting for?" "Pass it, pass it!" "Foul! That was a foul! The ref must be blind!" "Whew, that boy can fly!" one man cheers when his favorite player finally makes a basket.

Jazz music, loud voices, and laughter blend with the
buzzzzzzz of clippers and the soft *sweesh-sweesh* whisper
of scissors skimming loose hairs from a freshly cut head.

I look at the men in the row of chairs in front of me.
I can see their faces in the long mirror that runs along an
entire wall of the shop. The man in Mr. Seymour's chair
is getting his head shaved.
"Take it all off," he says.
A patch of sunlight gleams right on top of his bald head.

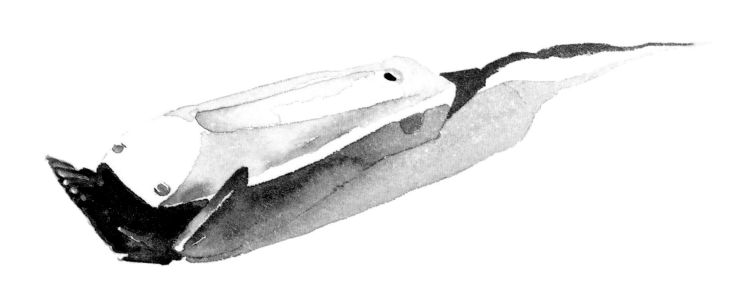

Another man has long, thick dreadlocks.
He's getting a shave with a straight razor.
When he leans all the way back in the chair,
his locks almost touch the floor.

The next man is getting his hair cut low all around.
The clippers go back and forth, dipping and gliding
across his head, making smooth waves that ripple
through his hair.

In the last chair, there's a kid, a little older than me,
getting his big, curly Afro trimmed. "Just a little off
the sides," he says.

But none of the styles I see look like me.

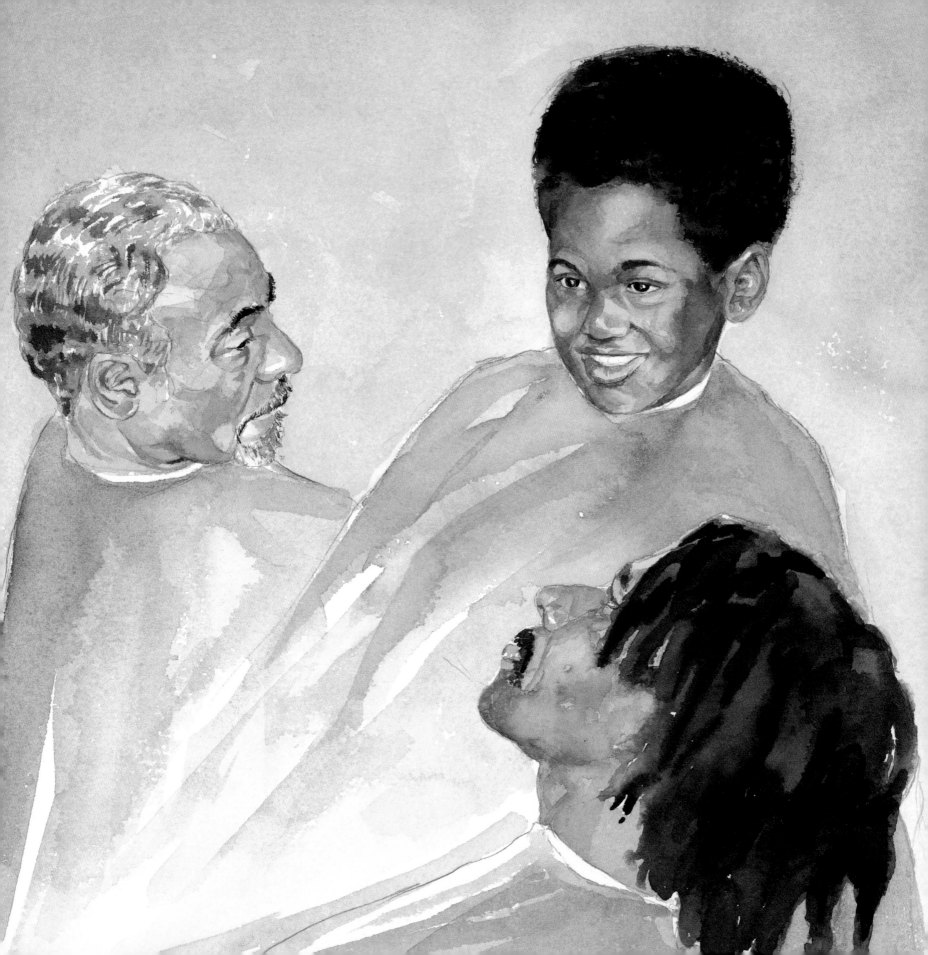

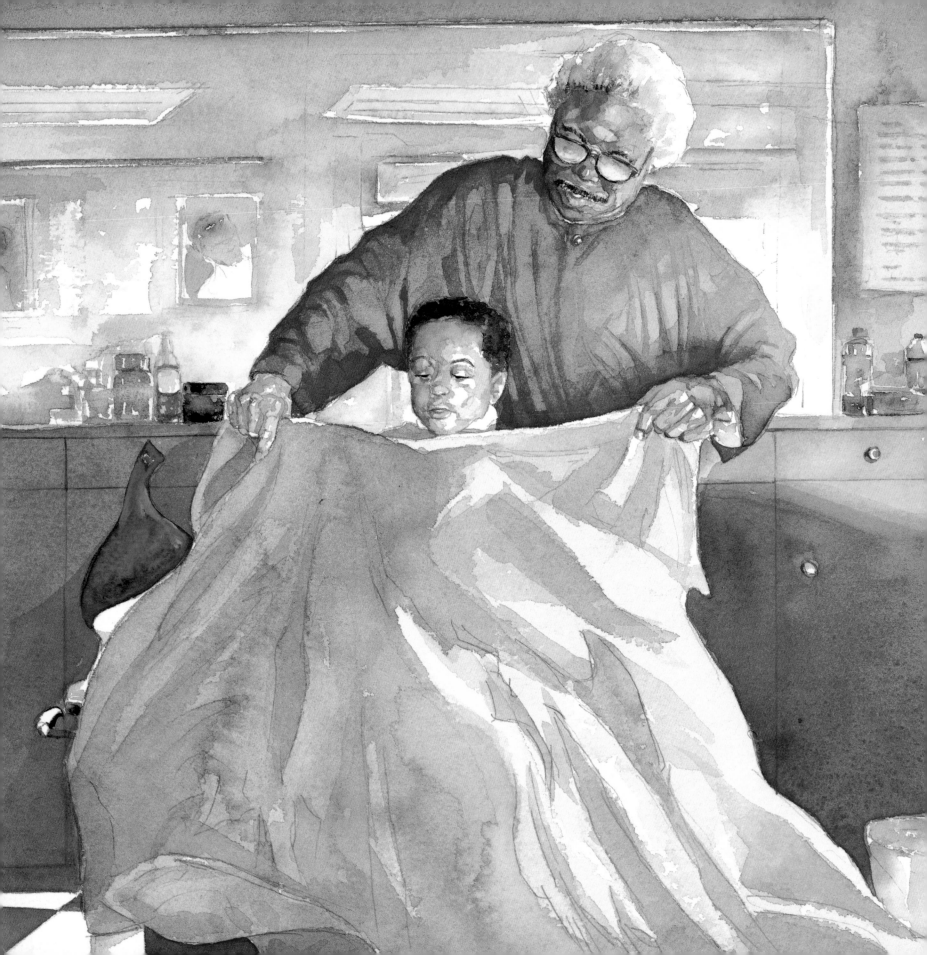

After a while, Mr. Seymour points toward Daddy and me and calls my name.

Me?!

I look at Daddy and then at Mr. Seymour and then at Daddy again.

"You go first, Miles," he says, and pats me on the shoulder. "Be brave, Little Man."

I can hear my heartbeat in my ears, and my knees feel wobbly.
But I stand up and walk over to the chair.

Mr. Seymour helps me up, the chair is so high.
Then he drapes a big, wide cape over me to catch the loose hairs.
"What style would you like for your first haircut, Little Man?" Mr. Seymour asks.
I shrug my shoulders. I don't know.

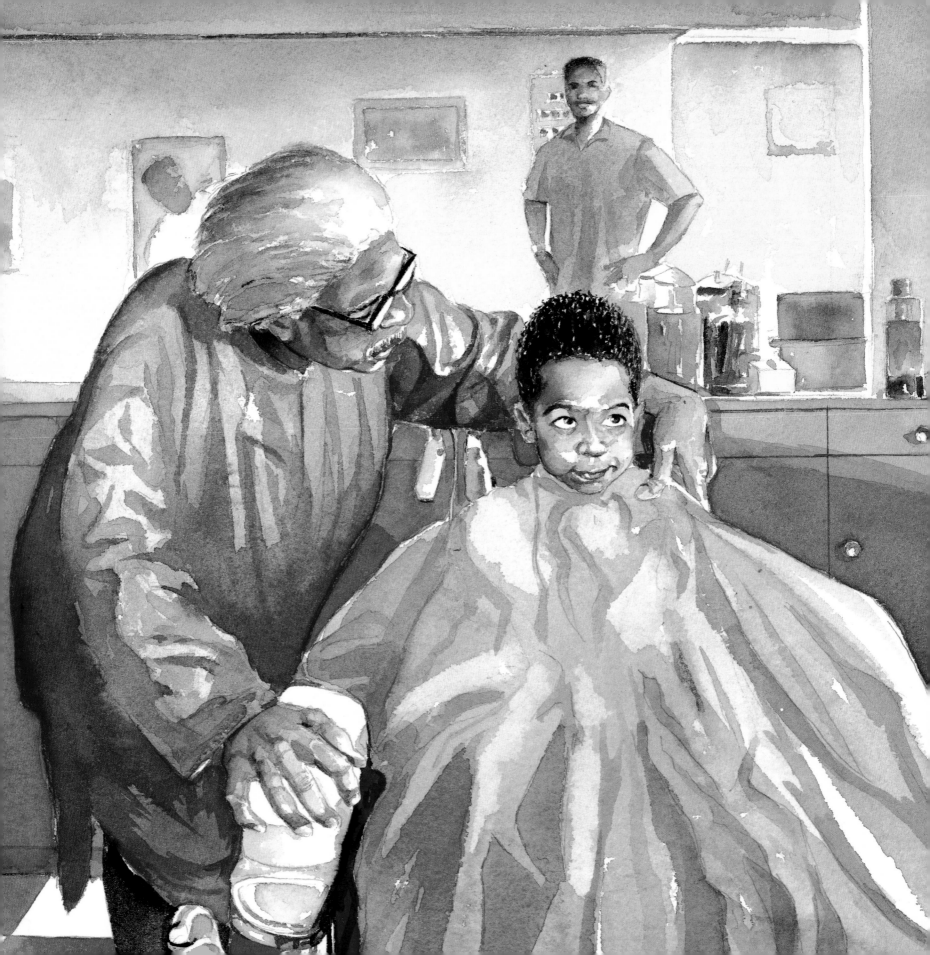

HAIRSTYLES

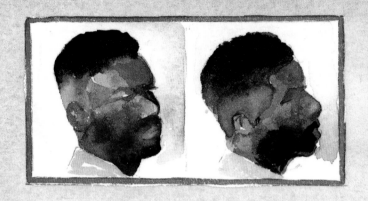 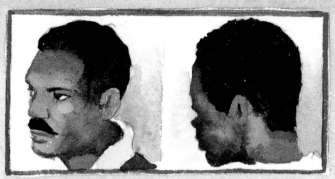

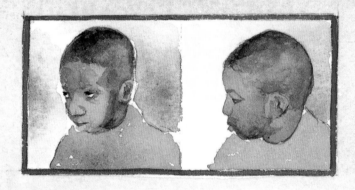

Mr. Seymour shows me a poster hanging on the wall
with pictures of all kinds of different styles, but I still don't see
any that look like me.

I take one more look around the shop, and when I see Daddy, I
know right away which style I want: cut low on top and shaved
clean all around, just like his.
I whisper to Mr. Seymour, and he goes to work.

Mr. Seymour takes out his pick.
He picks my hair until it is fluffy and stands up high.
Then, with his scissors, he begins to cut my hair
just like Mama used to do at home.

But when he finishes with the pick and scissors,
I hear him turn the clippers on.
My heart starts beating fast again.
*Will the clippers hurt? What if Mr. Seymour accidentally
cuts off my ear?*

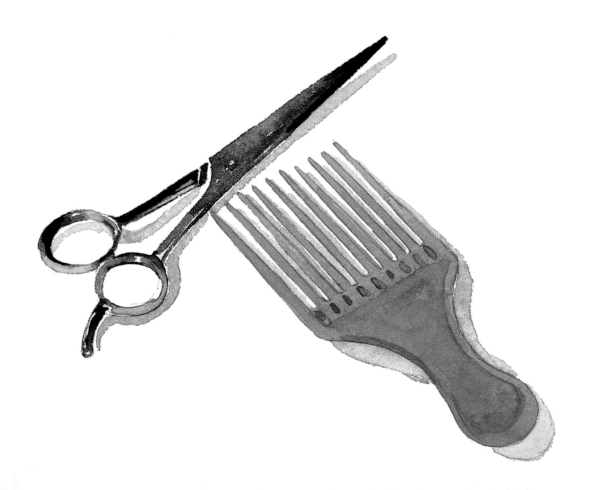

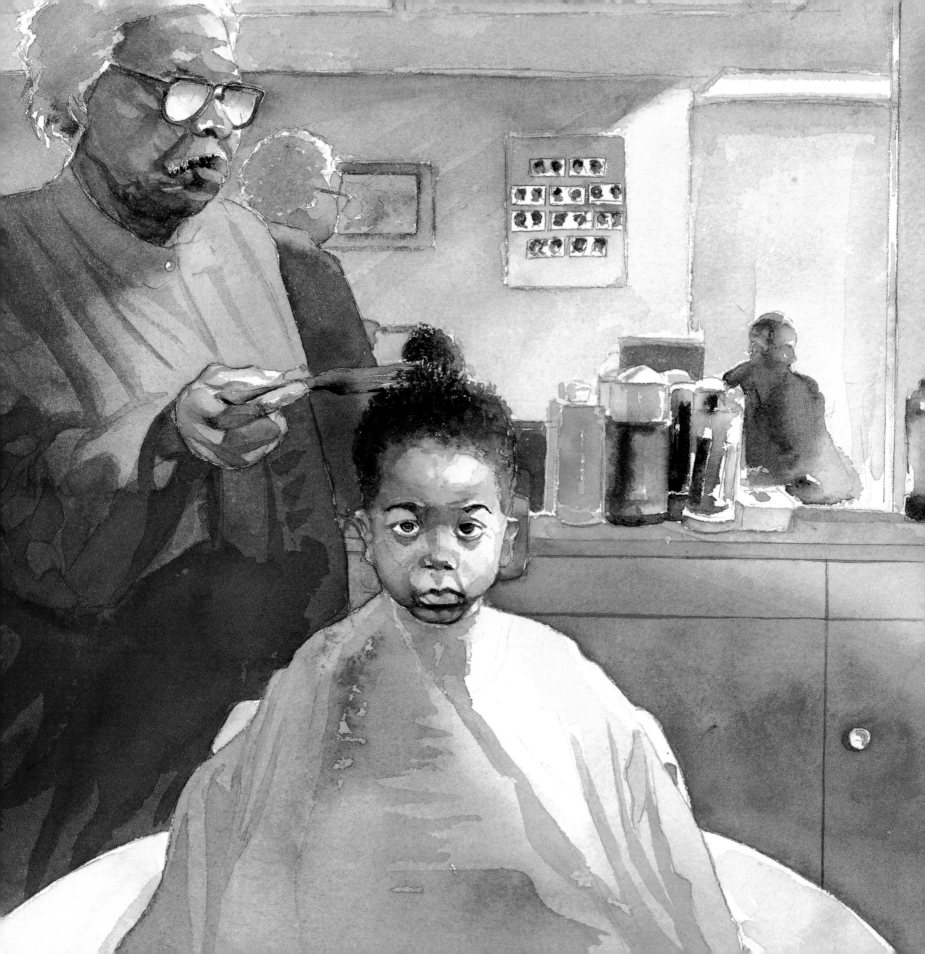

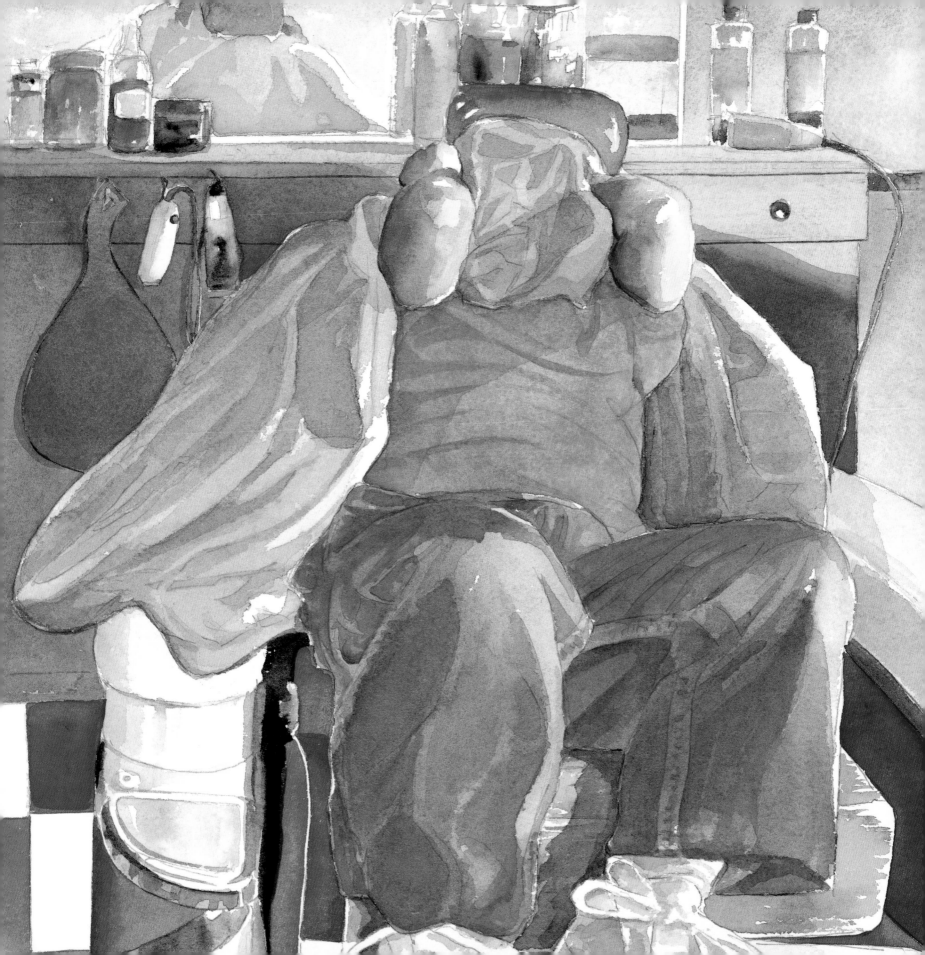

The loud buzzing noise is coming closer.
Then I feel a tickle creeping up the back of my neck.
I get so scared, I duck down as low as I can go in the chair and throw the cape over my head!

I peek out from under the cape when Mr. Seymour turns the clippers off. Daddy is squatting beside me. "I tried to be brave, but I didn't know how," I say with tears in my eyes.

"You know, I was scared when I
got my first haircut," Daddy says, and
wipes my tears away.
"You were?" I say with my eyes open wide.
Daddy nods.

"But I'll tell you a trick. Pretend that you're a giant, so tall
your head touches the sky. And the buzzing of the clippers is
just the sound of airplanes zooming by. Or maybe you're a
superhero, saving the earth from a swarm of killer bees. Try it. I
promise you won't be frightened anymore."

So I close my eyes and think about giants and my favorite superheroes.
But I can't picture any of them getting a haircut.
Then I remember watching Daddy get his hair cut,
the way he sits up tall and closes his eyes halfway,
like he doesn't have a care in the world.
I think about how brave Daddy is, and I get brave, too.

When Mr. Seymour turns the clippers back on,
I imagine that I have Daddy's long legs and wide shoulders.
I sit up straight like Daddy, though I still squeeze the arms of the chair tightly.

And when Mr. Seymour is through,
there is a brand-new me staring back from the mirror!

Mr. Seymour rubs a dab of a sweet-smelling blue
aftershave on my face and the back of my neck. It feels like a cool breeze.
Then he dips a brush in powder and gently sweeps it over my head and neck.

Daddy takes his seat in Mr. Seymour's chair.
And when Mr. Seymour asks him how he wants his hair, Daddy
says that he wants a haircut just like mine.
Daddy wants to look like ME!

When Mr. Seymour is finished, Daddy and I smile at each other
in the mirror.
"You sure we're not twins?" Daddy asks, raising one eyebrow.

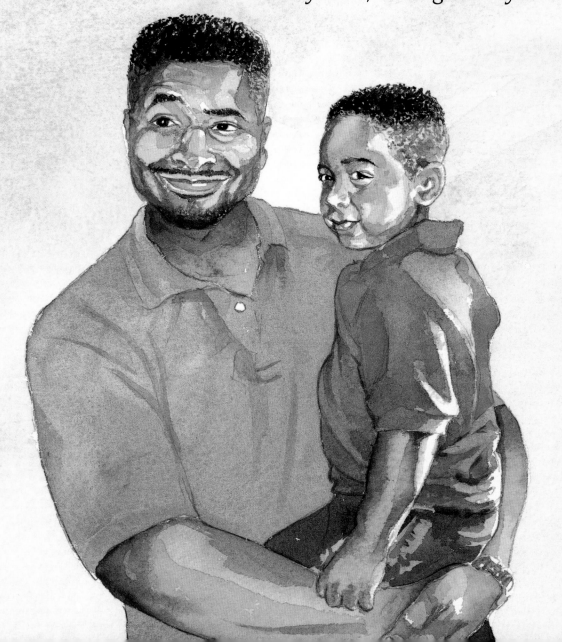

On the way out, some of the other men in the shop hold their hands up to me for high fives. "Looking sharp, man," they say. "Guess I can't call you Little Man anymore, Miles. You're one of the big boys, now," Mr. Seymour says, and shakes my hand. "See you next time."

I hum a happy, proud song as we leave Mr. Seymour's shop.
Bippity bop. Bippity-be-bop-bop.
Daddy picks up the tune.
We walk to the rhythm of our music, two cool cats, side by side.